SEP 3 0 2019

Note to Librarians, Teachers, and Parents:

Blastoff! Readers are carefully developed by literacy experts and combine standards-based content with developmentally appropriate text.

Level 1 provides the most support through repetition of high-frequency words, light text, predictable sentence patterns, and strong visual support.

Level 2 offers early readers a bit more challenge through varied simple sentences, increased text load, and less repetition of high-frequency words.

Level 3 advances early-fluent readers toward fluency through increased text and concept load, less reliance on visuals, longer sentences, and more literary language.

Level 4 builds reading stamina by providing more text per page, increased use of punctuation, greater variation in sentence patterns, and increasingly challenging vocabulary.

Level 5 encourages children to move from "learning to read" to "reading to learn" by providing even more text, varied writing styles, and less familiar topics.

Whichever book is right for your reader, Blastoff! Readers are the perfect books to build confidence and encourage a love of reading that will last a lifetime!

This edition first published in 2020 by Bellwether Media, Inc.

No part of this publication may be reproduced in whole or in part without written permission of the publisher. For information regarding permission, write to Bellwether Media, Inc., Attention: Permissions Department, 6012 Blue Circle Drive, Minnetonka, MN 55343.

Library of Congress Cataloging-in-Publication Data

Names: Koestler-Grack, Rachel A., 1973- author.
Title: Wood Ducks / by Rachel Grack.
Description: Minneapolis, MN : Bellwether Media, Inc., 2020. | Series: Blastoff! Readers. Animals of the Wetlands | Audience: Age 5-8. | Audience: K to Grade 3. | Includes bibliographical references and index.
Identifiers: LCCN 2018051145 (print) | LCCN 2018051557 (ebook) | ISBN 9781618915306 (ebook) | ISBN 9781626179905 (hardcover : alk. paper)
Subjects: LCSH: Wood duck--Juvenile literature. | Wetland animals--Juvenile literature.
Classification: LCC QL696.A52 (ebook) | LCC QL696.A52 K64 2020 (print) | DDC 598.4/123--dc23

Text copyright © 2020 by Bellwether Media, Inc. BLASTOFF! READERS and associated logos are trademarks and/or registered trademarks of Bellwether Media, Inc. SCHOLASTIC, CHILDREN'S PRESS, and associated logos are trademarks and/or registered trademarks of Scholastic Inc., 557 Broadway, New York, NY 10012.

Editor: Betsy Rathburn   Designer: Josh Brink

Printed in the United States of America, North Mankato, MN.

Table of Contents

Life in the Wetlands	4
Flying High	12
Diving for Food	18
Glossary	22
To Learn More	23
Index	24

Life in the Wetlands

Wood ducks are water birds that live in North America. These ducks are **adapted** to wooded wetlands.

They nest near streams, ponds, and **marshes**.

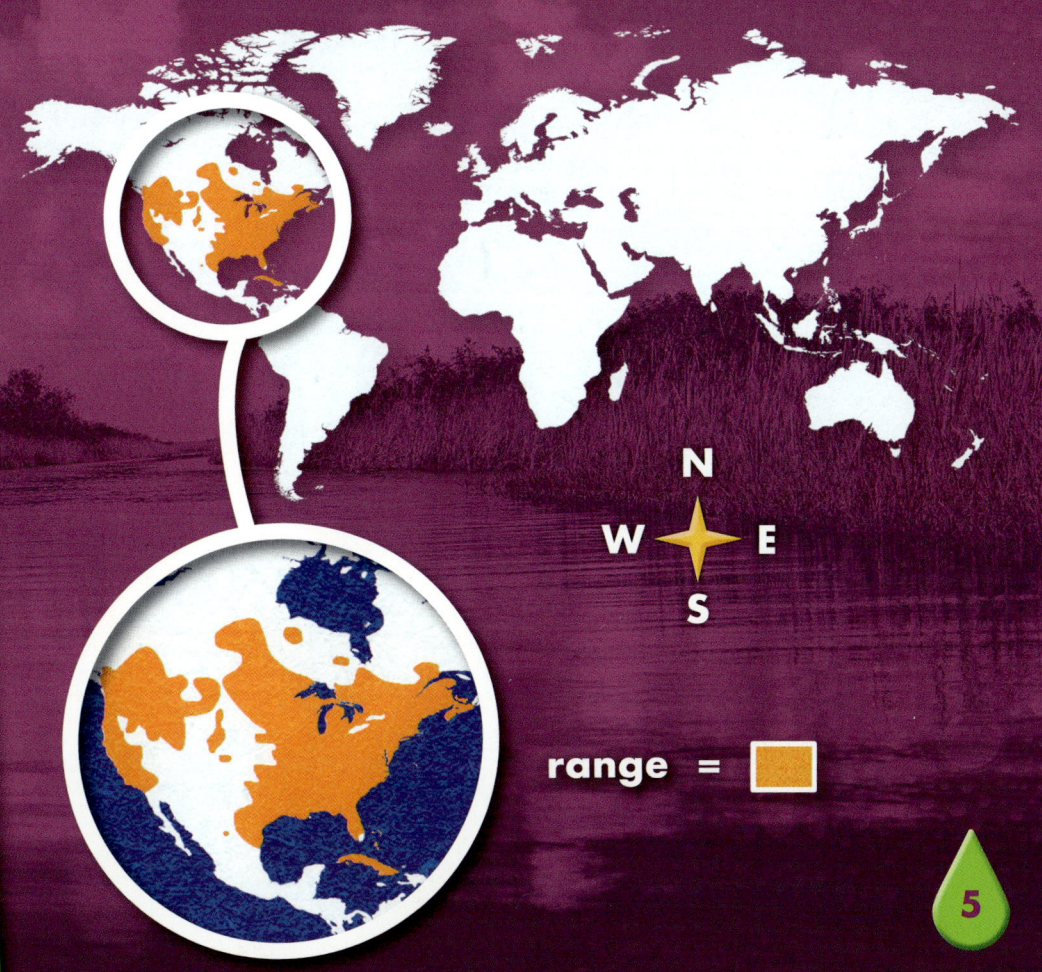

Wood Duck Range

range =

Wetlands are filled with water!
Wood ducks need to stay afloat.

Round bodies make them more **buoyant**. They paddle along with their **webbed** feet.

webbed foot

claws

Wood ducks spend a lot of time in trees. Sharp claws help them **perch** on branches.

Their short, wide wings easily twist and turn through thick forests!

Special Adaptations

webbed feet

short, wide wings

round body

Some wood ducks **migrate** north for the hot summer months. They head back south for winter.

Powerful wings help them fly long distances!

migrating

Flying High

The wetlands hold many **predators**. But wood ducks can often fly away!

When danger comes near, wood ducks speed to nearby trees or grasses.

These birds warn each other of danger, too. Sharp, squeaking calls tell other ducks to be careful.

Other calls help **mates** find one another in wide wetlands!

Wood Duck Stats

conservation status: least concern

life span: up to 15 years

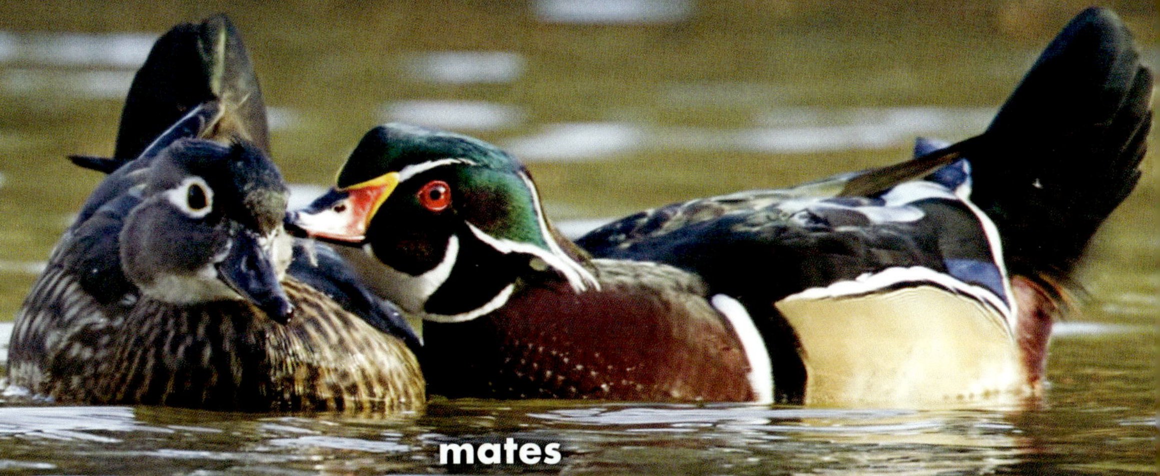

mates

female

Female wood ducks have **dull** feathers. This **camouflage** hides them from predators.

When danger is near, females keep their young safe. Ducklings hide near their mother!

Diving for Food

dabbling

Wood ducks are **dabbling** birds. They take short, shallow dives in search of food.

Water bugs and tadpoles become quick meals!

Wood Duck Diet

pill bugs

acorns

beech nuts

These water birds feast on land, too. They **forage** in nearby fields and forests. They especially like acorns!

foraging

Wood ducks **thrive** in the wetlands **biome**!

Glossary

adapted—well suited due to changes over a long period of time

biome—a large area with certain plants, animals, and weather

buoyant—able to stay afloat

camouflage—coloring or markings that make animals look like their surroundings

dabbling—dipping the head and bill underwater to hunt for food

dull—lacking color or brightness

forage—to search for food

marshes—low, grassy wetlands

mates—partners

migrate—to move from one place to another, often with the seasons

perch—to sit on a tree branch

predators—animals that hunt other animals for food

thrive—to grow well

webbed—having an area of skin between the fingers or toes

To Learn More

AT THE LIBRARY

Delano, Marfé Ferguson. *Ducklings*. Washington, D.C.: National Geographic Kids, 2017.

Gardeski, Christina Mia. *All About Wetlands*. Mankato, Minn.: Capstone Press, 2018.

Lawrence, Ellen. *Wood Duck*. New York, N.Y.: Bearport Publishing, 2017.

ON THE WEB

FACTSURFER

Factsurfer.com gives you a safe, fun way to find more information.

1. Go to www.factsurfer.com.

2. Enter "wood ducks" into the search box and click .

3. Select your book cover to see a list of related web sites.

Index

adaptations, 4, 9
biome, 21
bodies, 7, 9
calls, 14
camouflage, 16
claws, 8
dabbling, 18
danger, 13, 14, 17
dives, 18
ducklings, 17
feathers, 16
females, 16, 17
fields, 20
fly, 10, 12
food, 18, 19, 20
forage, 20
forests, 9, 20
grasses, 13
marshes, 5
mates, 14, 15

migrate, 10, 11
nest, 5
North America, 4
paddle, 7
perch, 8
ponds, 5
predators, 12, 16
range, 4, 5
seasons, 10
status, 15
streams, 5
trees, 8, 13
water, 6, 20
webbed feet, 7, 9
wings, 9, 10

The images in this book are reproduced through the courtesy of: Mia2you, front cover (background); Paul Winterman, front cover (wood duck); RudiErnst, p. 4; Oral Zirek, p. 6; Dolores Harvey, p. 7; Alberthep, p. 8; Silfox, p. 9; Dennis W Donohue, p. 10; Mircea Costina, pp. 11, 12, 17; Giacomo Parmeggiani, p. 13; Harry Collins, p. 14; Gregory Johnston, p. 15; Thye-Wee Gn, p. 16; Doris Dumrauf/ Alamy, p. 18; Marek Velechovsky, p. 19 (top left); Auhustsinovich, p. 19 (top right); PRILL, p. 19 (bottom); Antonia Gros, p. 20; Jim Nelson, p. 21; Tom Reichner, p. 23.

J 598.4 GRAC
Koestler-Grack, Rachel A.,
Wood ducks /

SEP 3 0 2019